SAM STICKS AND DELILAH

When Sam's parents split up, it looks like he will have to give away his dog Delilah. How can he persuade his father to let him keep her?

Diana Hendry is a poet and the author of numerous stories for young readers, including *Harvey Angell*, which won the Whitbread Children's Novel Award. She has also written the picture books *Dog Dottington* and *Christmas in Exeter Street*, the fiction titles *Wonderful Robert and Sweetie-pie Nell*, *Flower Street Friends* and *Fiona Says...* as well as the Walker Doubles *Hannah and Darjeeling* and *Midnight Pirate, Midnight Party*. She is also the author of novels for older readers, including *Double Vision* and *Minders*.

Also by Diana Hendry
Flower Street Friends
Hannah and Darjeeling
Midnight Pirate, Midnight Party
Wonderful Robert and Sweetie-pie Nell

For older readers
Double Vision
Harvey Angell
Minders

Picture Books
Christmas in Exeter Street
Dog Dottington

Sam Sticks
and Delilah

Diana Hendry

Illustrated by
Janet Duchesne

WALKER BOOKS
AND SUBSIDIARIES

LONDON • BOSTON • SYDNEY

First published in 1990 by
Julia MacRae Books

This edition published 1997 by
Walker Books Ltd, 87 Vauxhall Walk
London SE11 5HJ

2 4 6 8 10 9 7 5 3

Printed in England by Clays Ltd, St Ives plc

British Library Cataloguing in Publication Data
A catalogue record for this book is available
from the British Library.

ISBN 0-7445-5452-7

Contents

For John Henry

1 Banana Split

"That dog will have to go," said Mr Sticks.

He had said the same thing every night for a week now and every time he said it Sam got a lump in his throat.

It was supper time and they were eating baked beans and baked potatoes. There should have been sausages but Delilah had eaten them. For this she had been banished to her basket. There she lay, pretending to be sorry. (This wasn't easy – the pound of sausages had been very tasty.)

After supper, Mr Sticks slumped in his armchair with the evening paper and Sam went up to his bedroom. Delilah trailed after him, keeping one wary eye on Mr Sticks.

In his bedroom Sam picked up his violin. It was a very cheap one and he couldn't play it yet, but it had been a last present from his mother before she left. He tried to play a scale but it came out as a horrible screech and Delilah howled because she thought it sounded like cats.

With a sigh Sam put the violin back in its case and curled up on his bed. Delilah jumped up beside him.

"I won't let you go," Sam told her, "you're going to stay with me always."

Delilah licked Sam's nose, curled herself into a knot, nose to tail, and fell asleep.

Sam curled himself round her. She was as warm and comforting as a hot-water bottle. He tried to doze off but there was a sick, wobbly feeling in his tummy that kept him awake. What if his father meant it when he said Delilah would have to go?

It was true that Delilah was very naughty. Eating the sausages was just one of a number of crimes.

On Saturday she had jumped over the wall, gone missing and returned so muddy that Mr Sticks had to put her in the bath.

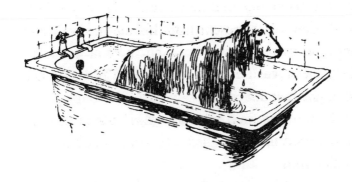

On Sunday she had discovered how to open the lid of the rubbish bucket. (They had found potato peelings all over the kitchen floor.)

On Monday she chewed up Mr Sticks's slippers.

On Tuesday she had learnt how to open the fridge door.

And today, Thursday, she had eaten the sausages.

Delilah was an Irish setter. She was only a year old and had not yet grown out of her puppy ways. She had been given to Sam by his parents on his eighth birthday.

She was a skinny, wriggling little creature with a dome on her head like a large egg. She had a plume of a tail and soft, floppy ears. Her fur was the dark red of autumn leaves. It made Sam feel warm just to look at Delilah. She was the best birthday present he had ever had.

Even when she was very small you could tell
that there was something wicked and adventurous
about Delilah. It was in the lilt of her tail. When
she pranced down the street on her long, unsteady,
puppy legs, Delilah's tail was like the plume on a
medieval knight's helmet. It waved in the air as if
to say, 'Here I come, world! It's me! Delilah! Make
way there!'

Delilah had only two moods. She was either very happy or very sad. Delilah was happy when it was meal time, when it was walk time, when she was lying in front of the fire or when she could sneak up beside Sam on the sofa. She was unhappy when she was left alone in the kitchen at night, when Mr Sticks got cross and thwacked her with a newspaper and when Mr and Mrs Sticks and Sam were eating – and she wasn't!

In the first few months of her life with the Sticks family, Delilah did a lot of naughty things. She chewed up shoes. She made muddy paw prints everywhere. Sometimes she made puddles on the kitchen floor. But none of that had mattered very much. Mrs Sticks had cleared up the puddles and washed away the muddy paw marks and taken Delilah out for walks in the afternoon while Sam was at school and Mr Sticks was at work.

But now Mr and Mrs Sticks had 'split' (that's what they called it at school) and everything had changed.

Sam did not like the word 'split'. It made him think of bananas sliced in half. Sam couldn't eat bananas any more. When he first heard the word he had thought of how he'd once split the seam of his jacket playing football and his mother had mended it. He wondered if you could mend a split between your mother and father. But it didn't seem likely. Mrs Sticks was living in the far north of Scotland with a man called Uncle Roger. She wrote Sam letters and said that he was to come and stay during the holidays. Sam hadn't dared to ask if he could take Delilah with him.

Nothing was the same since his mother had gone. It wasn't just that there were no nice smells coming from the kitchen when he came home from school. It wasn't simply that the fire was never lit or that Sam's T-shirts were never ironed. And it wasn't just that Sam's father always seemed grumpy. It was more as if all the sunshine had gone out of the house and left it cold and shivery. In fact since the 'split' everything and everyone had become horrid.

Except Delilah. It was Delilah who welcomed Sam when he came home from school. It was

Delilah who comforted him at night when she curled up in the bend of his knees. And it was Delilah who, when she waved the plume of her adventurous tail, cheered Sam up.

But on Friday morning Delilah leapt over the garden wall again and went streaking after a cat. Mr Sticks had to chase after her and made himself late for work.

And then he said it again, "That dog will have to go."

The lump came back in Sam's throat and his tummy went all wobbly. If he'd had a tail it would have hung very low that morning.

2 Is Happiness Catching?

There wasn't much time for breakfast because
Sam always took Delilah to the park before school.
Much as he loved Delilah, he didn't always feel
like going. It was December and at seven-thirty in
the morning it was still dark. The park, with its
avenues of trees, its empty swings and benches
looked ghostly.

Sam often had the feeling, as he went into the
park, that he was interrupting something – that
the trees had been moving about chatting to each
other and had hastily resumed their normal places
only when they saw him coming.

On his way to the park Sam could look in the
windows of all the neighbours' houses. Because it

was still dark, kitchen lights would be on and he could see families having breakfast – proper families with mothers and fathers who sat down at the table. (Sam and his dad ate bowls of cereal standing up.)

At number 55 he could see the Dobble family crowded round their kitchen table. Mr Dobble was opening a letter. Mrs Dobble was nursing the newest baby, several other Dobbles were eating toast. Maggie Dobble was waving her cereal spoon in the air. There always seemed to be dozens of Dobbles.

Mrs Dobble was a large, fat lady with uncontrollable hair. Her head was rather like a roundabout with lots of roads shooting off it. She seemed to collect children like other people collected stamps or jugs or beer mats. She had three of her own – Maggie, Bill and Norah – but she always had half a dozen others. "I've just borrowed this one," she would say, patting a stray child's head. Mrs Dobble was a foster mother. She looked after children when their own parents couldn't.

Sam hated the Dobble family. They always seemed so cheerful when he was miserable and he had the feeling that even in December there was a lot of sunshine in the Dobble house.

Most of all Sam hated Maggie Dobble. Maggie was in the same class as him at school. She had a round moon of a face, red hair, bright brown eyes and freckles across her nose. Maggie was a tom-boy. She wore trousers and a cap and in the autumn Sam had seen her in the park with the boys, tossing sticks up at the chestnut tree to bring down the conkers.

Whenever she saw him she always shouted out, "Here's Samson and Delilah!" and made everyone laugh. Sam hated that because he was not a bit like Samson in the Bible who was big and enormously strong and had lots of dark hair. Sam was skinny with thin pale yellow hair.

He always flushed bright red when Maggie called out, "Here's Samson and Delilah!"

At heart he knew that Maggie didn't mean any harm. She liked Delilah. She would always stop and stroke her and often she would beg Sam to let her take Delilah for a walk. (And sometimes she

saved a piece of chocolate for her.) But Sam
always said no and refused to let himself smile at
Maggie.

That morning Maggie saw him go past and ran to her front door.

"Samson!" she called. "Samson and Delilah!" Reluctantly Sam turned round. Delilah tried to pull him back towards Maggie.

"Can I come with you?" Maggie asked.

"No, you can't," said Sam. Delilah's tail sank very low.

"You're as cross as two sticks, Sam Sticks," shouted Maggie and slammed the door.

Sam could feel himself turning red again. He was glad there was no-one about except Mick, the paper-boy, wheeling about the silent streets on his bike. Sam liked Mick. He was always alone, like Sam.

When he reached the park he let Delilah off her lead and she bounded away. In the early morning light her plume of a tail gleamed dark red. Delilah never failed to find the park wonderful. She dashed in and out of the trees as if to say good morning to them all and to tell them how grand they were.

Sam felt happy just watching Delilah being happy. He wondered if happiness was catching, like measles. He found a stick to throw and Delilah chased after it, her ears whirling like the propellers of a helicopter.

Even though he felt better, Sam couldn't help thinking that it might have been fun to have Maggie with him. Delilah was excellent company of course, but she couldn't talk. But then, thought Sam, he would have nothing to say to Maggie Dobble. Although they lived in the same street and went to the same school and were near enough the same age, they came from two different worlds.

Maggie had a family. A big family. A whole banana family. Sam didn't think he could bear to hear her talk about her mother and father and

sister and brother when all he had was his dad
and Delilah. And how could he tell her how lonely
he often felt? And how he couldn't eat bananas for
thinking of banana splits? Anyway, he wasn't
going to have Maggie Dobble feeling sorry for him!

The park was not very big. It had a drinking
fountain in the middle that Delilah liked to drink
from and a paddling pool for the children and a
bowling green with a club house for people who
played bowls there in summer. Sam had seen them
there all dressed in white so that from a distance

they looked like a flock of sea gulls.

That morning he noticed that the door of the club house was open and it flashed into his mind that it would be a good place to hide. And then he heard the church clock clank eight o'clock and he called Delilah. She was over the other side of the park, investigating an abandoned gob-stopper. She came bounding towards him, stopped halfway and decided that it was a nice morning for a bath. She splashed happily into the paddling pool, swam across it, leapt out and shook herself all over.

Then dripping and bedraggled she came leaping across to Sam.

"Oh Delilah!" cried Sam. "Look at you!"

The paddling pool was not too clean. Delilah was sodden and dirty. They trailed home. Sam wondered if he could possibly find an old towel and rub Delilah dry before his father saw them.

Mr Sticks was in the kitchen ironing his shirt when they arrived. For a moment Sam felt sorry for his dad. Mr Sticks wasn't very good at ironing and he looked tired and worried.

Mr Sticks slammed down the iron when he saw them. (Delilah had shaken herself all over Sam so that his school shirt was spattered with mud.) Mr Sticks didn't say a word but his mouth went into a tight line and he rubbed Delilah down very roughly.

Sam knew what his father was thinking – "That dog will have to go."

3   A Serious Talk

That evening, after baked beans and baked potatoes (again), Mr Sticks said, "Sam, I want a serious talk with you."

Sam's heart sank. 'Serious talks' almost always meant something nasty. There had been a 'serious talk' before his mother left.

Mr Sticks sat down at the kitchen table looking miserable. Sam sat down opposite him. Delilah slunk under the table, and thumped her tail a few times to let them know she was there and settled down across Sam's feet.

"The thing is," said Mr Sticks, "everything has changed since your mother left and you and I have got to change too. I've got to learn to cook properly for a start." He gave Sam a small grin.

"I don't mind baked beans and baked potatoes," said Sam. (He didn't mind *anything* as long as Delilah could stay.)

"And I've got to learn to wash and iron – and make this place more like a home," said his father.

"I'll help," said Sam. "I can iron flat things like pillow cases."

Sam's dad nodded. "You're a great help, Sam," he said, "and I know life isn't easy for you at the moment but – well – it's Delilah I'm worried about. It's not fair to keep a dog cooped up in the house all day. Delilah needs a lot of exercise."

"It's all right in the holidays," said Sam.

"I know that," said his father. "But it's not all right the rest of the time. Particularly in the winter. Your mother used to take Delilah for a good long ramble in the country. But in the winter time it's too dark for you to go further than the park, and when I come home from work I'm too tired to go far."

"I could come home in the lunch hour," said Sam. He could feel the soft warm weight of Delilah across his feet. He lifted one foot carefully and stroked her head with his toe.

"No, you couldn't," said his father, "there isn't time for you to come home, walk Delilah *and* have your lunch. Also Delilah is getting naughtier and naughtier." (Delilah thumped her tail as if to deny this.) "It's because she's alone so much. Don't you think it would be fairer to Delilah if we found her another home? I know you'd miss her at first – but we could have a cat perhaps, or rabbits."

"I don't like cats or rabbits," said Sam. He was wondering if it was really true – if Delilah would be happier in another home. A whole banana home perhaps? He wanted to say that he'd eat beans and potatoes for ever if Delilah could stay and that he didn't care about the ironing and that it was Delilah more than all the cleaning and tidying in the world who made home, home.

But he couldn't say any of this because the lump in his throat was so large. Mr Sticks looked at his son and sighed. He loved Sam very dearly but he didn't quite know how to talk to him. Mrs Sticks had done that, along with the cooking and cleaning and mopping-up of puddles. He would have liked to give Sam a big hug, but somehow he felt too shy.

"Well," he said, "perhaps you'll think about it?"

He stood up and began to clear away the supper things. Sam went up to his bedroom and Delilah bounded happily after him.

Sam picked up his violin. He had the feeling that the violin could say some of the things that the lump in his throat stopped him from saying. The violin could speak of being sad and lonely. And it could lilt happily in much the same way as Delilah's tail could lilt. It could speak of the mysteries of the trees in the park. It could tell what it felt like being a banana split family. At least it could if he could play it. But all Sam could do was make it yowl and squeak. Delilah looked at him with a pained expression as if to say, 'Not cats again!' and crawled under the bed.

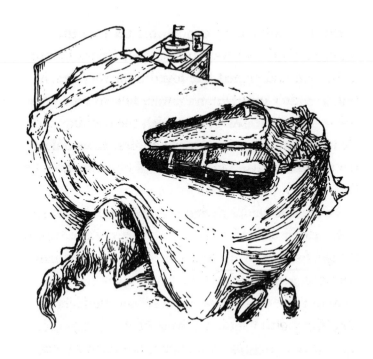

Sam put the violin down, lay on his bed and
cried. Delilah tried to lick away his tears.

"Oh Delilah!" said Sam putting his arm around
her neck. "You and I are never going to be split."
And suddenly into his mind came the picture of
the bowlers' club house in the park. He and
Delilah could go there and stay there! He would
get a paper round like Mick – several paper rounds

– then he could earn enough money to feed himself and Delilah. They would go for long, long walks and they wouldn't need to be a whole banana or a split banana family. They would just be a pair – Samson and Delilah.

He began to make a list of things he would take to the club house. A sleeping bag, Delilah's blanket from her basket, a saucepan and a knife, fork and spoon. With the list only half-made Sam fell asleep.

Downstairs in the kitchen Mr Sticks dried up the dishes and put them away. Maybe, he thought, without the expense of dog food for Delilah, he could buy Sam some violin lessons.

4 Running Away

Running away was easy. Sam got up early the next morning and, before his father was awake, he filled his knapsack with the things he needed. It was very heavy by the time he'd finished and he felt bad about taking the one and only tin-opener. His father would need it that night to open his tin of baked beans.

The thought of his father eating his baked beans all by himself almost made Sam change his mind. But then he looked at Delilah waiting for him with her head cocked on one side as if to say, 'What are you up to, Sam Sticks?' and he chose the oldest knife, fork and spoon from the drawer and put them in his knapsack.

He left his dad a note on the kitchen table. It said:

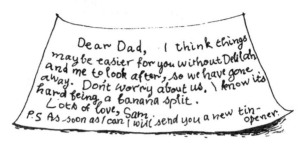

Dear Dad, I think things may be easier for you without Delilah and me to look after, so we have gone away. Don't worry about us. I know its hard being a banana split.

Lots of love, Sam

P.S As soon as I can I will send you a new tin-opener.

He slipped Delilah's chain collar over her head and attached the lead. Delilah's tail rose up in the air like a flag rising to the top of its pole.

It was still dark when they set off. No-one was about. It was too early for Mick the paper boy and even the Dobbles' house was in darkness. In the distance Sam could hear the whine of a milk float.

The knapsack on his back was heavy and he had to stop every now and again to ease his shoulders. "Samson," he said to himself. "Samson and Delilah! That's us."

There was no-one in the park of course. The trees seemed to huddle together, shaking their tops at each other as if in astonishment at seeing a human being so early in the morning.

Delilah was delighted by the emptiness of the park. She dashed around in circles three times before rushing up to Sam so fast that she skidded to a halt like a car with sharp brakes.

It began to rain. Sam thought of his father coming down into the kitchen and reading the note. There was something nice about his father when he came downstairs in his pyjamas, his hair all tousled and his face still crumpled from sleep. His still-sleepy face was a much nicer face than his straightened-out-and-important office face which he wore after he'd washed and shaved and dressed.

Sam headed for the club house. He'd brought a marmalade sandwich with him. He would dump the knapsack in the club house, make some kind of a home – a sort of nest maybe – for him and Delilah, eat his marmalade sandwich and plan what to do next.

But when he got to the club house it was locked! A new bolt had been fitted and a padlock and chain added. Sam put down his knapsack and rattled it furiously – helplessly. All the trees shook their heads at him. 'It's all right for you!' Sam wanted to shout at them. 'You're just one big happy family!'

He walked all round the club house to see if there was a window open but there wasn't. It was raining quite heavily now. Delilah sat and watched Sam. Her ears drooped like large, wet cabbage leaves.

Sam took shelter under the Lebanon cedar. The Lebanon cedar was the largest tree in the park. Its branches spread wide like a giant umbrella.

Sam crouched down under the tree. It was dry under there but gloomy. What if this were his only home, this dark umbrella under which nothing grew? Tears came into his eyes. He thought of his mother in Scotland. Scotland was an awfully long way away. He had no idea even which direction to go in and he had no money for food until he got the paper round.

There was nothing for it but to go home. They trailed miserably back, both of them soaking wet. Sam tried to work out how he could do a paper round *and* walk Delilah in the morning. And how

long it would take him to earn enough money to run away properly?

He began to hurry now. It was important to get home before his father saw the note. The Dobbles were up when he hurried past their house. Maggie Dobble pushed up her bedroom window and called out to him – "Been swimming then, Sam Sticks? Come and have breakfast at our house."

"No thanks," said Sam stiffly. "My breakfast will be waiting for me." This was an awful lie and as he said it a picture of bacon and eggs rose before his eyes. He'd be lucky if his father had remembered to buy another packet of cereal. Shopping was another thing Mr Sticks wasn't much good at.

They just about made it. As he opened the back door he could hear his father's alarm clock ringing, then some groans and mutters, the creak of the bed and the pad of bare feet going to the bathroom.

Sam shoved the knapsack into the kitchen
cupboard, grabbed the note and scrumpled it up
and was towelling Delilah dry when Mr Sticks
came downstairs. He expected his father to be
angry about the kitchen floor and yet another wet
towel, but instead Mr Sticks took the towel from
him and said, "Here! I'll do that. You go and have
a hot bath. You look like a drowned rat. I'm going
to make some porridge. That'll warm you up."

Surprised, Sam went off for a bath. When he came downstairs there was a warm bowl of porridge on the table and Mr Sticks was grilling bacon. Sam sat down and ate the porridge. It was a bit lumpy but he didn't mind. It was warm and it filled the hollow in his tummy. It was a funny kind of hollow, as though being hungry was like being lonely and both gave you the same kind of empty feeling. The bacon was rather undercooked but Sam ate most of it and put the scraps in Delilah's bowl.

Then, after tying up the fridge door (so Delilah couldn't get into it), and putting the rubbish bucket on top of the fridge (so Delilah couldn't reach it), Sam went off to school and Mr Sticks went off to work and neither of them said anything about Delilah having to go. But the thought was there, and it stood between them like a large and invisible wall.

5   The Sharers

That night Mr Sticks made cottage pie. It was rather dry and the carrots were a bit hard but it was a nice change from baked beans and baked potatoes. Also there was a doughnut each and a bottle of lemonade.

"I was wondering," said Mr Sticks when they had finished all but the smallest corner of the cottage pie (saved for Delilah) and were on to the doughnuts, "if you would like some violin lessons?"

Sam sat straight up at the thought. Would he? Oh he would! Then he paused and looked carefully at his father. Something was going on, thought Sam – porridge for breakfast, cottage pie and doughnuts for supper and now the chance of violin lessons. Was it all a bribe? Would his father at any moment say, "Now, about Delilah . . ."

"I'd love violin lessons if we could afford them," said Sam cautiously.

"Well, we'll see," said Mr Sticks, licking doughnut sugar off his fingers. "Now then, about Delilah."

Here it comes, thought Sam, and he put down the rest of his doughnut. He wasn't hungry any more.

"I had a chat with a friend at work," said Mr Sticks, "and he came up with a really good idea."

Sam kept quiet. Nothing that took Delilah away from him was a good idea. "Yes," continued Mr Sticks, "he suggested we share Delilah."

"Share her!" echoed Sam astonished. "How d'you mean 'share her'? She's mine!"

"Yes, yes, I know that," said Mr Sticks soothingly (he thought of the knapsack he had found in the kitchen cupboard and the scrumpled up note), "this house is mine but we could share it – we could take in lodgers for instance. We are sharing this table. You could share the rest of your doughnut with me – if you wanted to."

Sam frowned. Homes, tables, doughnuts – they were all very different from a dog and very different indeed from *his* dog, Delilah. Sam couldn't think of anything worse than sharing Delilah. Well, almost nothing.

"But why?" he asked. "And who would we share her with?"

"If you think about it," said Mr Sticks, "there are probably lots of families who would like to own a dog but can't afford one – dogs are quite expensive to keep – particularly big dogs like Delilah. And if Delilah had somewhere to go while we were out – and someone else who'd take her for a walk and look after her during the daytime – well, it would make everything much easier, wouldn't it?"

"Yes," said Sam reluctantly.

"Things can't go on like this," said Mr Sticks. "We've got to do something and this seems like a really good idea to me."

"Who would we – er – share – her with?" asked Sam sulkily.

"I thought we'd advertise," said Mr Sticks, "in the post office window. Lots of people advertise there for all sorts of things – home helps, rooms to rent, lost cats."

Sam finished off the doughnut. The main threat of losing Delilah altogether seemed to be over. If his father's plan worked he wouldn't have to run away after all.

"All right, then," he said. "As long as these – these sharers know that it's just a loan."

"We could put a label on her tummy like they do with library books," said Mr Sticks grinning. "Return by 4.30 Tuesday afternoon!"

Sam couldn't help but laugh at the idea of
Delilah with a library label on her tummy. Mr
Sticks found an old envelope and began writing
out the advertisement for the post office window.
When he finished it looked like this:

Sam drew a picture of Delilah underneath the
words.

All the same Sam had terrible dreams that
night. He dreamt of dreadful sharers – cruel dog
beaters and nasty tail-pulling children. He kept
waking up hot and scared, but Delilah, at the
bottom of his bed, thumped her tail and snored.
Comforted, Sam fell asleep again.

In the morning Mr Sticks took the
advertisement to the post office on his way to
work. "If someone Delilah doesn't like comes
along we can always say no," said Mr Sticks to
Sam who was still looking worried.

The porridge had improved that morning.

"You're getting to be quite a good mum!" said Sam and to his surprise his father gave him a hug.

As things turned out, it was someone *Sam* didn't like who knocked on the door that evening and said politely, "I've come about Delilah. We could give her lots of love and attention – and walks." Delilah wagged her tail at the very word 'walks' but Sam scowled. For there on the doorstep stood Maggie Dobble.

A very pleading Maggie Dobble. She clasped her hands together and gazed up at Mr Sticks with her big brown eyes and Sam could see his father melting on the spot. Nor was Delilah much help. She remembered Maggie Dobble's chocolate.

"Now let's see," Mr Sticks was saying, "you're one of the Dobbles, aren't you? From across the road? Very convenient don't you think, Sam?"

Sam growled.

"That's right, Mr Sticks," said Maggie. "There are five of us – well mostly five, sometimes six or seven – well, never more than ten. And we'd love a dog. We've been wanting one for ages and ages. And Delilah knows me already, don't you, pet?"

"I can see she does," said Mr Sticks smiling, "and she likes you, too!"

Maggie beamed.

"Well, Sam and I will talk it over and I'll come and see your mum," said Mr Sticks.

"Rightie ho," said Maggie and to Sam's fury she gave him a wink. "Bye Samson," she said. "Bye Delilah. Bye Mr Sticks," and she ran off down the road.

Mr Sticks slapped Sam on the back.

"Well there you are, Sam," he said. "I think we've found the perfect sharer!"

6 A Whole Banana Family

Despite all Sam's protests, the Dobbles became the dog-sharers. The only other person to reply to the advertisement in the post office was a little old lady who took one look at Delilah and said, "Oh no! I wanted to share a small dog."

And in any case, Sam couldn't put up a very good case *against* the Dobbles. All he could say was, "I don't like that Maggie Dobble. She's always teasing me."

"Maybe you haven't been very friendly," said Mr Sticks. Sam and Mr Sticks went over the road to talk to the Dobbles about sharing Delilah.

It felt funny to Sam, being inside the house of the whole banana Dobble family rather than looking through the window at them. It always looked so friendly and happy from the outside. But inside it was rather different.

Two of the smallest foster children, Daniel and Elizabeth, were having a terrible quarrel about a game of *Snakes and Ladders*. The fire had gone out and Bill Dobble was trying to get it going again. And Mrs Dobble was on the telephone when the tiniest Dobble swallowed a sweet whole and began to choke. Mrs Dobble dropped the telephone, turned the child upside-down and banged him on the back until the sweet shot out. When he was right-way up again he looked very red-faced and weepy and Mrs Dobble gave him his blankie to cuddle.

Sam gave his father a look as if to say, 'There! I told you so! The Dobbles could never look after Delilah!' But Mrs Dobble shook hands with Mr Sticks and within minutes she produced tea and biscuits.

"I'll call a pow-wow," said Mrs Dobble and she put two fingers in her mouth and blew a piercing whistle. (Sam really envied that whistle.) Within minutes, all the Dobbles had gathered together in the living room.

"Sam and Mr Sticks have come about dog-sharing," said Mrs Dobble.

Every face in the room was turned towards Sam and Mr Sticks.

"We've wanted a dog for years," said Bill Dobble shyly. "I could easily take her for a walk in the lunch hour – my school's only round the corner."

"She could have my scraps," said Norah.

"Norah has rather a lot of scraps," said Mrs Dobble. "I can take Delilah for walks, too. The little ones like going to the park in the afternoon. We can take Delilah with us."

"And I'll give her love and attention," said

Maggie and everyone laughed.

"Well, I think that's settled then," said Mr Sticks. "I'll bring Delilah over here when I go to work and Sam will collect her when he comes home from school."

"And maybe I can come with you to the park in the mornings," said Maggie to Sam. "Just sometimes."

Being shared suited Delilah down to the ground (or up to the tip of her happy tail). Every morning she was eager to be off to the Dobbles and every afternoon she was delighted when Sam came to collect her. She had three walks a day. One from Sam (and sometimes Maggie), one from Bill and one with Mrs Dobble. She had two sofas to curl up on and lots of people telling her how beautiful she was. And the scraps at the Dobble house were (thanks to Norah) very good indeed.

As they got used to sharing Delilah, they all grew friendlier. Bill and Sam swapped books. Sam kept the stamps off his father's letters for Norah Dobble who collected them.

Sometimes when he came home from school, Sam stayed and had tea with the Dobbles and afterwards they all played *Monopoly*. And sometimes Mrs Dobble gave him a pie to take home to his father.

During the holidays there always seemed to be one or other of the Dobbles over at Sam's house, and if Sam didn't take Delilah over to the Dobbles, her tail began to droop and she sat on a chair by the window looking very miserable.

The lonely-hungry feeling in Sam's tummy went away and when he went to visit his mother in Scotland, he didn't have to worry about Delilah. He knew his dad and the Dobbles would look after her.

But he was still uncertain about Maggie Dobble. It was true she didn't tease him any more and she didn't nag him (well, not often) to let her come with him to the park. No, what bothered Sam was that of all the Dobbles, Maggie seemed to be Delilah's favourite. Whenever he took Delilah round to the Dobbles' house, Delilah always looked for Maggie. And it was Maggie's bed – out of all the Dobble beds – that Delilah chose to lie

on. It's just that she gives her chocolate, Sam told
himself. But he knew that wasn't really true.

Delilah and Maggie were alike. They both had
red hair and they were both either very happy or
very sad. When Maggie walked up the street she
had the same hopeful and adventurous look that
Delilah had.

"You mustn't spoil Delilah," Sam said to
Maggie.

"I don't!" said Maggie, tossing her head.

"You're always giving her chocolate," said Sam.

"Only once a week – as a treat," said Maggie.

Then to his surprise Maggie lost her temper. "You're a miserable old stick, Sam Sticks," she shouted. "You've got two homes and a dog and you get all the attention in the world because there's just one of you. You don't have to share any of your toys or your bedroom – or anything! If it wasn't for me Delilah would be shut in all day, all miserable and lonely!" And with that Maggie burst into tears and ran from the room, banging the door behind her.

Sam went home thoughtfully. He had never thought of himself like that before – a boy with two homes (one in Walnut Street and one in Scotland), lots of attention and a dog of his own. It hadn't occurred to him that Maggie could feel jealous of a boy from a split banana family as he felt jealous of a girl from a whole banana family.

"I'll be nicer to her tomorrow," he said to himself.

But he didn't see Maggie the next day.

"She's very poorly," said Mrs Dobble. "I think it's flu. You'd better not see her in case you catch it."

7 Sam and Samson

Maggie made an awful patient. She lay in bed and felt hot and then shivery. She felt hungry and then sick and she was very sorry for herself indeed.

For the first day or two of Maggie's flu the other Dobbles weren't allowed to do more than pop their noses round the door and say, "Hi, Maggie! Get better soon," because Mrs Dobble said she couldn't cope if everyone got flu. Usually Maggie shared a bedroom with Norah, but Norah had been moved into Mrs Dobble's room when Maggie was poorly.

Sam missed seeing Maggie. He missed her coming to the park with him. He missed seeing her at school. He missed her cheerful wave and her red hair. Maggie's red hair was like Delilah's red fur, he thought – it made you feel warmer on a cold day.

He was hoping that on the third day, when he went to collect Delilah, Maggie would be feeling better and he could go and see her.

He wasn't exactly planning to say 'sorry' to Maggie for being a miserable old stick – oh no, he wouldn't go as far as that. But somehow he'd show her that he *was* sorry and that he did like her.

But when he got to the Dobbles' house, Maggie was still in bed. Mrs Dobble was at the ironing board in the kitchen with a mountain of ironing in a big wicker basket beside her. From up above Sam could hear the sound of someone crying. Maggie!

"I've been with her all afternoon," said Mrs Dobble, trying to get a wandering country-lane of hair back to the roundabout of her head, "but I simply must get this ironing done. She's lonely, that's the trouble. And she say it hurts her head to read and she misses Norah in her bedroom."

Sam stood first on one foot and then on the other. What he had to say wasn't easy.

"Do you think it would help if – if Delilah stayed the night with her?" he asked. And then, because Mrs Dobble had put down her iron and was looking at him in astonishment, he added, "She's really very comforting curled up on your bed at night – I'm sure she'd make anyone feel better."

And then it was Sam's turn to be surprised for Mrs Dobble came over and gave him such a big hug he thought he was going to be squashed to a match-stick.

"Sam Sticks," said Mrs Dobble, "I think that is a very kind thought. I think Delilah would make Maggie feel lots better. Probably do her more good than all the medicine in the world. Would you like to pop your nose round the door and tell Maggie

that Delilah can stay?"

"No – that's all right. You can tell her," said Sam, for he felt rather shy.

But on the way home, alone, without Delilah, he suddenly felt very warm and happy inside. It had been a hard thing to do but Mrs Dobble had been pleased. She'd given him that great squashing hug. Sam felt somehow stronger – as if inside skinny Sam Sticks there really was a Samson.

"Where's Delilah?" asked Mr Sticks when he came home from work.

"Oh, she's staying with Maggie tonight," said Sam as if it hadn't cost him any heartache at all. "Maggie's not very well. I thought Delilah would make her feel better."

Mr Sticks raised his eyebrows in surprise. "Well," he said, "that was kind of you." And Sam blushed and felt Samson-like again.

"I've found you a violin teacher," said Mr Sticks, "and I've booked you a lesson."

"That's great," said Sam. "That's kind of *you*!"

"No, it's not," said Mr Sticks. "Delilah and I can't stand those caterwauling screeches any more!"

Of course it was very odd being without Delilah that night. But the next afternoon when he went over to the Dobbles' house and saw Maggie sitting on the sofa in her dressing gown with Delilah curled up beside her, he was glad he had done it.

Delilah jumped off the sofa, bounded up to him and licked his face all over. Maggie laughed. "You won't need a bath tonight," she said. "Would you like a game of *Ludo*?"

Sam said he would and they sat on the rug before the fire. Delilah jumped back on the sofa and stretched herself out.

"Now she's really pleased with herself," said Maggie, "she's got the whole sofa to herself and she doesn't have to share it with anyone."

"She doesn't know what she's missing," said Mrs Dobble. And Sam thought so too.